williambee
Stanley's
Garage

MOTOR

OIL

Ω

Published by
PEACHTREE PUBLISHERS
1700 Chattahoochee Avenue
Atlanta, Georgia 30318-2112
www.peachtree-online.com

Text and illustrations © 2014 by William Bee

First published in Great Britain in 2014 by Jonathan Cape,
an imprint of Random House Children's Publishers UK
First United States version published in 2014 by Peachtree Publishers

The illustrations were rendered digitally

Printed and bound in March 2014 by Leo Paper Products in China

10 9 8 7 6 5 4 3 2 1
First edition

Library of Congress Cataloging-in-Publication Data

Bee, William, author, ilustrator.
Stanley's garage / by William Bee.
pages cm
ISBN: 978-1-56145-804-2
Summary: "Stanley is working at his garage today. From filling up Hattie's red sports car with gas to changing
the tire on Shamus and Little Woo's blue car, it sure is a busy day. As his friends each come in with their car
problems, Stanley knows just what to do to get them back on the road."— Provided by publisher.
[1. Automobile repair shops—Fiction. 2. Hamsters—Fiction. 3. Rodents—Ficton.] I. Title.
PZ7.B38197Sv 2014
[E]—dc23
                                              2013049353

williambee

Stanley's
Garage

PEACHTREE
ATLANTA

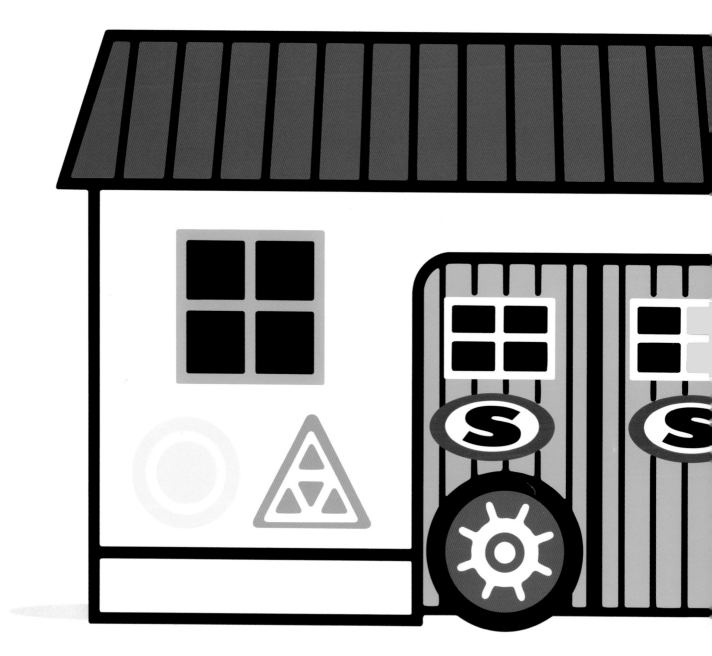

This is Stanley's garage.
Who will drive in today?

Here is Stanley's friend Hattie.

She needs some gas for her
red sports car.

And here are Shamus and Little Woo.

Oh no! Shamus's blue car has a flat tire.

Stanley jacks the car up. He changes the flat tire for a nice round one.

Shamus and Little Woo say,
"Thank you, Stanley!"

Now what is causing all this smoke?

It's Charlie's yellow car. It's overheating.

Stanley quickly fills the radiator
with cold water.

Ring! Ring! Ring! Ring!
Stanley's telephone is ringing.
It's Myrtle. Her car has broken down
on the way to the store.

Stanley drives out in his tow truck.

He tows Myrtle's purple car—and Myrtle—
back to the garage.

Stanley puts Myrtle's car up on the lift.
Stanley gets very oily,
but he fixes the problem.

And off Myrtle goes!
Thank you, Stanley!

Well! What a busy day!

Time for supper!
Time for a bath!

And time for bed!
Goodnight, Stanley.

Stanley

If you liked **Stanley's Garage** then you'll love these other books about Stanley:

Stanley the Builder
Stanley's Diner
Stanley the Farmer